First published by Parragon in 2012
Parragon
Chartist House
15–17 Trim Street
Bath BA1 1HA, UK
www.parragon.com

Edited by: Gemma Lowe
Designed by: Jim Willmott
Production by: Jack Aylward

ISBN 978-1-78186-036-6

Printed in China

Bath • New York • Singapore • Hong Kong • Cologne • Delhi
Melbourne • Amsterdam • Johannesburg • Shenzhen

One day on Shipwreck Beach, Cubby is playing his harmonica.

"Aw, coconuts! I'll never be ready in time to play at Marina's party," says Cubby sadly.

"I don't care what you say, Smee!" says Captain Hook.
"I do not need a – yawn – nap."

"Oh, Cap'n," says Smee, "you know how
cranky you get when you don't have
your nappy-nap."

"All right, Smee," says Hook.
"A little nappy might do me
good."

Hook is drifting off to sleep
in his hammock, when suddenly
he is startled awake by the sound
of music!

"One of those puny pirates is making an awful racket with his blowy music thing!" says Hook.

"Why don't you ask the sea pups nicely if they'll be a little quieter?" says Smee.

"Smee, who do you think you're dealing with?" says Hook. "Why would I ask nicely when I can take the blowy thing away!"

"Yay-hey, that's the way!" says Izzy. "You're getting better already, Cubby!"

"You'll be a harmonica master in no time," says Skully.

"Not if I can help it!" calls Captain Hook.

Hook uses his fishing hook to snatch the harmonica right out of Cubby's mouth!

"My harmonica!" says Cubby.

"We gotta get it back!" says Jake.

"Who would've thought that great big noise could come from this tiny little thing?" says Smee.

Smee blows into the harmonica.

It makes a terrible noise!

Startled, Smee throws the harmonica up in the air … but it doesn't come back down!

"Um, Cap'n," says Smee, "the harmonica just disappeared!"

"I don't care if it sprouted wings and flew away," says Hook, "so long as I have peace and quiet for my nap."

"Crackers!" says Skully. "That monkey took the harmonica!"

"Mr Monkey, may I have my harmonica back, please?" asks Cubby.

"Oo-oo!" The monkey swings off into the Never Jungle.

"I'd take that as a no," sighs Skully.

"He's heading for the Never Jungle," says Cubby.

"Come on, crew," says Jake. "Follow that monkey!"

"But how?" asks Cubby.

"Monkey see, monkey do," says Jake.

"Great idea," says Izzy. "We can swing on the vines just like the monkey!"

"Wait for me," calls Cubby.

"Uh-oh," says Skully. "I've lost sight of the monkey!"
"He could be anywhere in this jungle," says Cubby.
Just then, the crew hears music!
"It's my harmonica," says Cubby.
"Follow that sound," says Jake.

"Hi, Mr Monkey," says Jake. "I'm glad you like the harmonica, but it belongs to my friend Cubby."

"And I need it to practise for the big party tonight!" adds Cubby.

"Oo-oo-OO," says the monkey, crossing his arms.

"He doesn't want to give the harmonica back," says Izzy.

"If only we had another instrument," says Jake. "Then we could trade with the monkey."

"That's a great idea," says Izzy.

"But we don't have another instrument," says Cubby.
"Not yet," says Izzy. "But we can make an instrument for the monkey to play." Izzy picks up two coconuts.
"Now we need something to put inside," says Izzy.

"I've found some rocks," says Cubby.
"I've got some shells," says Skully.
"How about some sand?" says Jake.
"Perfect," says Izzy.

Shake-a, Shake-a, Shake-a!

"Awesome! You've made some maracas for the monkey," says Jake. The monkey gives Cubby back his harmonica.

"Thanks!" says Cubby. "Hey, do you wanna come back to Shipwreck Beach and jam with me?"

"Oo-oo-oo," says the happy monkey.

Cubby and the monkey play music together on the beach!

"Blast it, now there's twice as much racket!" says Captain Hook.

"What's the matter?" asks Jake.

"The Cap'n can't have his nappy-nap, what with all that music," says Smee.

"Why didn't you just ask us to be quieter?" asks Jake.

"But, how can I practise for the party?" says Cubby.

"I've got an idea," says Jake.

Cubby and the monkey play a gentle lullaby for Captain Hook. Mr Smee sings:

"Cap'n, close your weary eyes.
Now it's time for beddy-byes.
The music's sweet, it's not too shabby.
When you wake up, you won't be crabby."

Hook falls asleep and starts to snore!
"We'd better get ready for the party," says Jake.
"What? I can't hear you over all that noise," says Skully.

Later that night, Cubby and the monkey play their instruments at Marina's party!

"Cubby, thank you so much for playing," says Marina. "You were amazing!"

"You're welcome," says Cubby, blushing.

"Yo-ho, way to go!" says Jake. "See? All that practising paid off!"

"Can't you hear it, Smee," says Captain Hook.
"Hear what, Cap'n?" asks Smee.
"That blasted lullaby. I can't get it out of me head," says Hook.
"Oh, dear, you're imagining things, Cap'n," says Smee.
"I guess I am," says Hook.
"I can see why. It was a catchy tune, if I do say so myself," says Smee. "And the lyrics were top-notch."
Uh-oh! The monkey has stowed away on the *Jolly Roger*!

"If Hook had just asked us to be quiet, we wouldn't have gone through all that trouble today," says Jake.

"Yeah, Hook should know better! If you need something, you should ask nicely," says Izzy.

"Yeah, but if the monkey didn't take the harmonica, we never would've gotten to jam together!" says Cubby.

"Check it out! For solving pirate problems today, we earned some gold doubloons," says Jake.

"Let's count 'em," says Cubby.

"We earned eleven gold doubloons," says Jake. "Yo-ho, way to go!"